Good Night Cowboy

Glenn Dromgoole

Illustrated by

Barbra Clack

BRIGHT SKY PRESS

Good night boots.

Good night hat.

Good night cow dog

and barn cat.

Good night pony. Close your eyes.

We'll ride tomorrow, you and I.

Good night tractor in the shed.

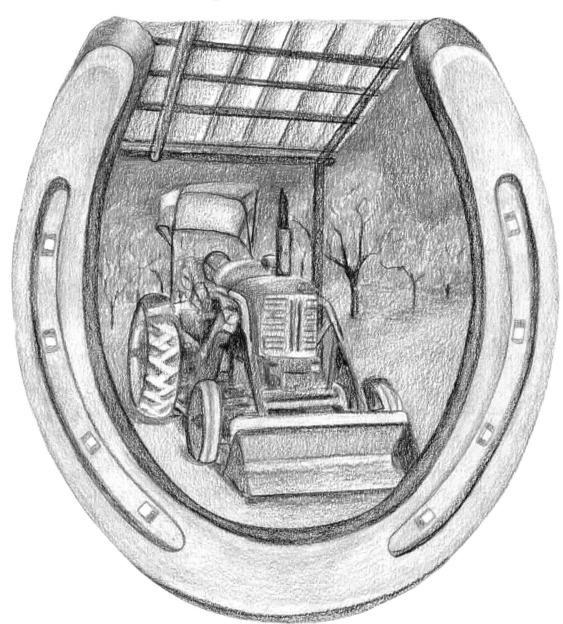

Good night cattle. You've been fed.

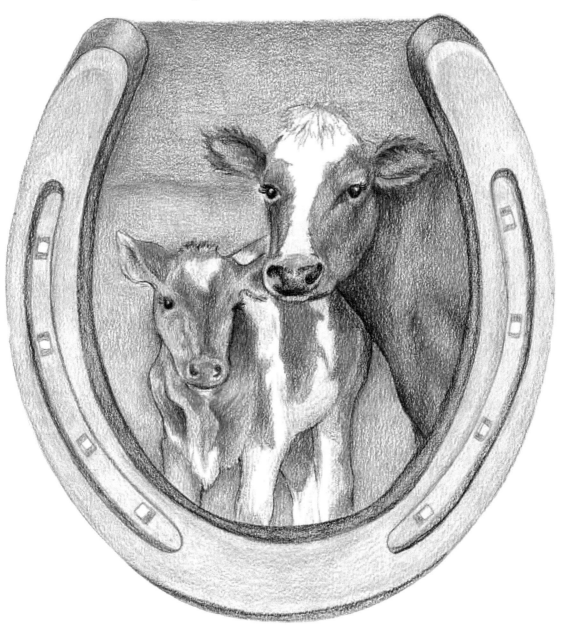

Good night windmill, fence and pen.

Good night rooster. Good night hen.

Good night flowers, cactus, trees,

Grasses blowing in the breeze.

Good night jackrabbit and horned toad.

Armadillo, crossing the road.

Good night mountain,

Prairie and plain,

Good night soft clouds.

Good night rain.

Good night sunset in the western sky.

Good night stars so bright and high.

Good night friends and family, too.

Good night cowboy—

I love you.